READ THIS FIRST!!!

Most books are about other people.

This book is about you!

What happens to you depends on what you decide to do.

Do not read this book from the first page through to the last page.

Instead, start at page one and read until you come to your first choice. Then turn to the page shown and see what happens.

When you come to the end of a story, go back and try another choice. Every choice leads to a new adventure.

Have fun at the circus!

THE CIRCUS

EDWARD PACKARD

ILLUSTRATED BY PAUL GRANGER

A BANTAM SKYLARK BOOK®
TORONTO • NEW YORK • LONDON • SYDNEY • AUCKLAND

RL2, 007-009

THE CIRCUS
A Bantam Skylark Book / November 1981

ISBN 0-553-15120-7

Published simultaneously in the United States and Canada

PRINTED IN THE UNITED STATES OF AMERICA

0 9 8 7

THE
CIRCUS

It's summertime, and the circus is in town. You'll be the first one to see it! Your Uncle Harry and Aunt Alice are circus people. They've invited you to visit before the show begins.

Aunt Alice is an acrobat. She walks on a tightrope and swings on the trapeze. Uncle Harry trains polar bears.

Turn to page 2.

2   Aunt Alice and Uncle Harry are waiting for you at the big tent.

"Welcome to the circus!" Aunt Alice says. "We're glad you're here. Now you can learn all about circus life. You'll even have a chance to be in the show."

"What would you like to do most in the circus?" asks Uncle Harry. "Would you rather be an acrobat, an animal trainer, or a clown?"

If you say that you would **3**
like to be an acrobat,
turn to page 4.

If you say that you
would like to be an
animal trainer,
turn to page 6.

If you say that you would
like to be a clown,
turn to page 8.

4   You say that you would like to be an acrobat.

Aunt Alice points to a long tent pole that is lying on the ground. "Can you walk from one end to the other without falling off?" she asks.

Step by step, you are able to walk the whole length of the pole.

"You have good balance," says Aunt Alice. "Are you ready to climb to the top of that rope ladder?"

You crane your neck back. Your eyes follow the ladder, way, way up to the very top of the circus tent. It sure looks high up.

Are you ready to climb it?

If you think you are ready, turn to page 11.

If you just want to stay on the ground, turn to page 26.

6   You tell Uncle Harry that you would like to be an animal trainer. He takes you to a steel cage on the other side of the main tent. Inside the cage is the biggest polar bear you've ever seen.

A workman is standing at the door of the cage. He holds a thick pole in one hand and a bucket of fish in the other.

"I'm teaching this bear to shake hands," says Uncle Harry. "Would you like to watch me? Or would you like to meet The Great Kamchatka and his famous lions? Or would you like to see where the animals live—behind the big tent?"

If you tell Uncle Harry that you'd like to watch him train the polar bear, turn to page 13.

If you say that you would like to meet The Great Kamchatka and his famous lions, turn to page 18.

If you say that you would like to see where the animals live, turn to page 21.

8   "I really want to be a clown," you say.

Aunt Alice takes you to see Charley the clown. Charley bends down to shake your hand. "Goodbye," he says.

You wonder why Charley said "goodbye" instead of "hello." Then you notice that his coat is on backwards and his hat is upside down.

"Charley likes to surprise people," Aunt Alice says. "He never says what you expect him to say."

Charley smiles at you. "Would you like to be in one of the acts in today's show? I drive around the arena in a mini-car. Everyone thinks there is only one person in the car. Then lots of clowns and kids jump out. You could be part of the mini-car act. Or you could be the eight-foot-high ostrich."

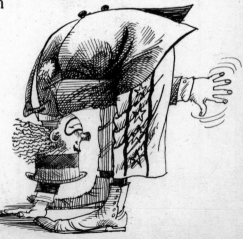

If you want to be in the mini-car act, turn to page 45.

If you want to be the eight-foot-high ostrich, turn to page 22.

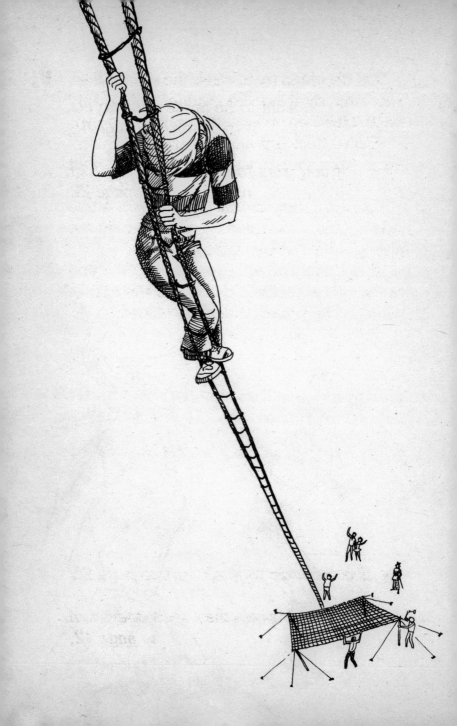

You decide to try to climb the rope ladder.
You start climbing. The ladder swings and twists. Half way up, you stop and look down.

"Don't think about how high you are," Aunt Alice calls. "Just think about what you're doing!"

You keep climbing to the very top of the ladder. You look down again. Two men are rigging a big net beneath you.

"You're safe now," Aunt Alice calls. "You can jump all the way down into the net, or you can climb back down the ladder."

If you decide to jump, turn to page 25.

If you climb down the rope ladder, turn to page 12.

12   "I'd rather have a job where I can stay on the ground," you call to Aunt Alice.

As you hop down from the ladder, Uncle Harry walks over. "Would you like to learn how to train lions?" he asks.

If you say "yes," turn to page 18.

If you say "no, thanks!," turn to page 36.

You tell Uncle Harry that you would like to **13** watch him train the polar bear.

Uncle Harry steps inside the cage and cracks his whip. The bear sits down and holds out his paw. Uncle Harry waves it up and down. The bear doesn't seem to mind. Uncle Harry gives him a fish.

"It takes a lot of patience to train animals." Uncle Harry turns to look at you. "Some day this bear will be able to dance and play ball, but—"

"Watch out!" you yell.

The bear has jumped from his seat! Uncle Harry starts to turn, but the bear swipes at him with his huge paw. Uncle Harry goes flying across the cage and lands up against the bars.

Turn to page 16.

Chuck smiles. "Hank could teach school if **15** he could talk!"

"Ask him how much eight take away five is," you say.

Once again Chuck looks Hank in the eye. "Hank, what is eight minus five?"

Nothing happens for a few seconds. Then Hank slowly taps his hoof three times—the right answer again!

Uncle Harry takes you to see the rest of the circus. You like every bit of it, but nothing seems quite as amazing as Clever Hank, the smartest horse in the world.

The End

16 Quickly the workman pokes the bear with his pole. The bear growls, but backs away. Uncle Harry jumps to his feet and lets himself out of the cage.

"I forgot the main rule of bear training," he says. "Keep your eye on the bear!"

"It's like *keep your eye on the ball*," you reply. And right then you decide that you would rather play ball than train bears.

The End

18   Uncle Harry takes you to meet "The Great Kamchatka." He is a big man with flashing brown eyes and a black beard. He leads you to a large cage. Inside the cage are six lions. Each lion is sitting on a stool. One is yawning. Another is licking his chops. The others stare at you. They look ready to jump.

You watch Kamchatka pick up a big hoop and hold it in front of one of the lions.

"Jump!" he calls in a sharp voice. The lion jumps through the hoop.

"Sit!" The lion jumps onto his stool.

Kamchatka keeps his eyes on the lions while he calls to you. "Would you like to come in the cage with me for a minute? You'll be quite safe. Just don't let the lions think you're afraid."

If you go inside the cage, turn to page 30.

If you say "no, thanks," turn to page 32.

You tell Uncle Harry that you'd like to see what's behind the main tent. He leads you through the rear doors into a large yard where the big circus trucks and vans are parked. One of them has a sign that says, "CIRCUS ANIMALS—KEEP BACK."

You stop for a moment in front of a bear cage. A small white bear is watching you through the bars. He looks as gentle as a lamb. You would like to pat his soft, furry head.

Uncle Harry has walked on ahead.

If you reach through the bars and pat the bear, turn to page 27.

If you catch up with Uncle Harry, turn to page 29.

22   Charley the clown brings you an ostrich costume. It looks like a big black coat with white feathers. You put it on, and Charley zips it up. Then he leads you to a tall mirror. You can see yourself through the eyeholes. Now you're an ostrich—but with no legs!

Charley tells you he'll be right back. When he returns, he is holding your "ostrich legs."

"Now you have to learn to walk on stilts," he says.

You take the stilts and practice standing on your "ostrich legs." After a while, you are ready to walk. You strut around the ring.

Charley claps his hands. "You're a great ostrich," he says. "How would you like to be in today's show?"

If you decide to be the ostrich in today's show, turn to page 51.

If you decide just to watch the show, turn to page 52.

You leap off the high platform and fall toward the net—faster and faster and faster. You hit the net so hard it takes your breath away. You bounce high into the air, land again, roll to the edge of the net, and hop to the ground. The workmen cheer!

"No doubt about it," says Aunt Alice. "Pretty soon you'll be able to walk on a tight rope and swing on the trapeze! Would you really like to learn to be an acrobat?"

If you say that you want to be an acrobat, turn to page 34.

If you'd rather be a clown, turn to page 8.

26 "I think I'm afraid of high places. I'd rather do something else," you say.

"O.K.," says Uncle Harry. "I don't like heights myself." He leads you out of the big tent and points to a sleek, black horse with a white star on his forehead. "That's Clever Hank, the smartest horse in the world."

Hank lifts his head out of a bucket of oats and looks at you. A man wearing chaps, a bright red vest, and a cowboy hat, walks up to you.

"Meet Chuck Collins," says Uncle Harry. "He's Hank's trainer. Some people say that he's almost as smart as Hank!"

"Is Hank really the smartest horse in the world?" you ask.

"Watch," says Chuck. He steps closer to Hank and looks him in the eye. In a slow, clear voice he says, "Hank, what is two plus three?"

Hank slowly taps his right front hoof five times.

Turn to page 15.

You reach in and pat the bear on the head. He feels like a big, furry dog.

Suddenly, you feel a sharp tug on your arm. The bear has your arm in his mouth, and his huge teeth are pressing into your skin! You try to pull away, but the bear won't let go.

You cry out. Uncle Harry runs toward you. He throws some pepper in the bear's face. The bear sneezes. You sneeze too. But now your arm is free.

Uncle Harry looks closely at the tooth marks on your arm. "You're lucky," he says. "Another few seconds and you might have lost an arm. Now you'll never forget the first rule of bear training—*Never trust a bear!*"

The End

You run to catch up with Uncle Harry. He **29** shows you the red and gold vans that carry the animals. He points to a row of trailers. "The circus people live in those trailers. That big truck over there carries the tents, ropes, chairs, and everything you can think of. . . ."

"TIGER LOOSE!" A woman is screaming! "HELP!" someone cries. Uncle Harry runs around the big truck toward the noise.

But the tiger has come around the other side of the truck. It is walking slowly toward you. It reminds you of a cat looking for a mouse, but this time *you* are the mouse!

There's no time to think. What will you do?

If you just stand there, turn to page 42.

If you run for your life, turn to page 41.

30 Kamchatka's helper opens the door to the lions' cage. You slowly step inside.

One of the lions growls. He jumps down from his stool.

Crack! Kamchatka cracks his whip. *"Sit!"*

But this time the lion will not sit. Kamchatka cracks his whip again, but the lion crouches as if ready to spring. He starts toward you. You try to open the cage door. It's stuck!

Crack! goes the whip. *"Sit!"* Kamchatka cries.

"*SIT!*" you shout at the top of your lungs. In a flash the lion jumps back on his stool!

Uncle Harry opens the door, and you dart out of the cage. "You must be the youngest lion trainer in the world," he says.

Later Uncle Harry takes a picture of you

and the great Kamchatka. You'll never forget the day you went into the lions' cage!

The End

32   "Maybe you would rather work with the sea lions," says Kamchatka. "We have six of them. They play basketball."

"I'd like that," you reply.

Kamchatka takes you to the pool. The sea lions half swim and half slide through the shallow water. They bounce the ball off one another's noses.

Kamchatka gives you a ball, and you **33** throw it to a sea lion. He bounces it back to you.

You play with the sea lions for most of the day. You only wish that you could take them all home.

The End

"I'd like to learn to be an acrobat more than *anything*," you tell Aunt Alice.

"That's great," she says. "But it will take lots of practice. Why don't you stay with us for awhile?"

You call home. Good news! You can stay with Aunt Alice and Uncle Harry for most of the summer.

You practice hard every day. You learn how to walk on a tightrope and how to stand on your hands. After awhile, you can swing and climb like a monkey.

Go on to page 35.

Most of all,
you like to
stand on the
shoulders
of a boy who
is standing
on the
shoulders of
a small man
who is
standing on
the shoulders
of a medium-
sized man
who is
standing on
the shoulders
of the
biggest man
in the circus!

The End

"No, thanks,"
you call to Uncle
Harry.

"I don't blame
you," says Aunt
Alice. "Nothing
would make me
go into a lion's
cage!"

"Nothing would
make *me* walk on
the high wire,"
says Uncle Harry.

They offer you two other choices.

If you'd like to hold the safety rope for the trapeze artist, turn to page 38.

If you say you don't know what you'd like to do, turn to page 48.

38   Aunt Alice takes you to
meet some of the acrobats
in the main ring.

A pretty
woman waves
from her trapeze
high above you. Her costume sparkles in the
light as she swings back and forth. A rope
goes from her harness to a tiny wheel at the
top of the tent. From there it runs all the way
down to the floor.

"I'm Maria," the woman calls to you.
"Will you please grab that safety rope? Then,
if I fall, I will come down gently."

You take the rope and watch her swing
higher and higher. She holds on with only
one hand as she swings round and round.

Suddenly you feel a hard tug on the rope.
Maria has lost her grip! She's falling! Since
you're holding the other end of the rope, *you*
start to *rise.*

Turn to page 40.

40   You hold the safety rope tightly as you rise quickly into the air! It seems as if you will go through the roof!

Finally you stop rising. But you are still high in the air! You look down. Maria has landed on her feet and is holding the other end of the rope.

"Hold on! I'll let you down," she calls. But you are already sliding down the rope.

You reach the ground safely. Maria shakes your hand. "Thanks for saving me," she says. "Now you're an acrobat too!"

The End

You run through the yard, screaming. **41**
Never have you run so fast. Never have you
yelled so loudly.

Now Uncle Harry is chasing the tiger. But
the tiger is chasing you, faster and faster. You
feel his hot breath on the back of your neck.
You look around. His great jaws open
wide. . . .

Turn to page 44.

42   You stand very still.

Step by step, the tiger comes toward you. His green eyes gleam. His mouth opens. A great red tongue rolls out between huge pointed teeth.

You notice a red tank on the wall next to you. On the tank is a label. It says,

POINT HOSE AT BASE OF FIRE.
THEN PULL THE WIRE LOOP.

The tiger moves closer . . . and closer. You grab the tank and pull the loop. A fountain of white spray fills the air. The tiger rears up with an angry roar, then turns and runs behind the big truck.

A minute later Uncle Harry returns, a smile on his face. "Quick thinking!" he tells you. "The tiger went back into his cage. No one was hurt. Today you're the star of the circus!"

The End

The tiger is gone! You are sitting in your own bed. It is nighttime. Then you remember. . . . You were at the circus this afternoon. The tiger didn't chase you. It was only a dream.

Thank goodness!

The End

You've always wanted to know how so **45** many people fit inside that tiny car, so you decide to be part of the mini-car act. You are a little scared, though. Will you be crushed by all those people?

Before the show begins, Charley leads you to a hiding place under the floor of the arena. Other clowns and circus kids are waiting there. One kid has a big, fierce-looking dog on a leash.

"That's Fang, our circus mascot," says Charley. "He's part wolf and part Husky dog."

"Will he be in the car, too?" you ask.

"He sure will," says Charley.

Turn to page 46.

Soon a bell rings. It's time for the mini-car act to go on. A trap door swings open above you. Charley sets a ladder up against it.

"Follow me," he says. Then he races up the ladder, climbs into the car, and jumps out through the car door. You and *everyone* else follow behind him. You all run out of the big

tent. Fang chases Charley, howling like a wolf. The crowd laughs and cheers.

Afterward, you have a party with the clowns and the other kids. It's been a great day for you at the circus!

The End

48 "I'd rather have another job," you say, "but I'm not sure what else there is to do."

"Well," says Uncle Harry, "right now there's only one other job left. It's the first job I had when I joined the circus."

You follow Uncle Harry to the yard behind the main tent. You walk past the wild animal cages and the horse vans. Then Uncle Harry picks up a shovel and a pail and hands them to you.

"Here's what you need for your job," he says. "Someone has to clean up after the elephants. Now it's your turn!"

"Oh, no!" you say.

The job isn't fun at all, and it's pretty smelly. You're glad when you've finished it, because the show is about to begin!

Turn to page 52.

Charley the clown asks you to wait behind
the big tent. Soon the band begins to play.
Then you hear Charley whistle. "It's your
turn!" he calls.

You get up on your stilts and walk into the
ring. The people cheer. You strut around
and wave your ostrich head at the children in
the front rows.

Suddenly you lose your balance. You're
falling!

CRASH!

You look up at the stands. Everyone is
laughing. You feel like crying.

You slowly get back up on your stilts and
walk out of the tent and into the rear yard.
Charley is waiting for you there. He pats you
on the back.

"I'm sorry I did such a bad job," you tell
him.

"You may not be such a good ostrich,"
says Charley, "but you're a very good
clown—because you made everyone laugh.
And that's what clowns are supposed to do!"

The End

52 Charley the clown shows you to your seat. The stands are filled with people. Men with white jackets and straw hats are walking up and down the aisles. *"Popcorn, peanuts, cotton candy . . ."* they shout.

The band begins to play. The trombones blare. The brass horns go *Oom Pah, Oom Pah, Ooom Pah, Ooom Pah.* Three fat clowns follow, beating a big bass drum.

The proud horses gallop into the ring.

They are dressed in satin robes covered with **53**
shining beads. Red, blue, and green lights
shine down from the roof.

The lights dim. A spotlight shines on the
Ringmaster. He is dressed in a white suit with
a tall white hat. He sings the song, *Hi, Neighbors! Hi, Neighbors!*

"The circus is about to begin," Charley
whispers to you. "We think it's the greatest
show of all!"

The End

READ THIS LAST!!!

While you were reading this book, did you happen to read page 15? If so, you may have wondered whether Clever Hank was really able to add and subtract.

Hank was a smart horse, all right, but he wasn't *that* smart. He couldn't really add and subtract, but he knew that he was supposed to stop tapping his foot when his trainer smiled. And his trainer always smiled whenever Hank had tapped his foot the right number of times!

ABOUT THE AUTHOR

EDWARD PACKARD, a graduate of Princeton University and Columbia Law School, practices law in New York City. He developed the unique storytelling approach used in the CHOOSE YOUR OWN ADVENTURE™ series while thinking up bedtime stories for his three children.

ABOUT THE ILLUSTRATOR

PAUL GRANGER is a prize-winning illustrator and painter.

Now you can have your favorite **Choose Your Own Adventure®** Series in a variety of sizes. Along with the popular pocket size, Bantam has introduced the **Choose Your Own Adventure®** series in a Skylark edition and also in Hardcover.

Now not only do you get to decide on how you want your adventures to end, you also get to decide on what size you'd like to collect them in.

SKYLARK EDITIONS

☐	15238	The Circus #1 E. Packard	$1.95
☐	15207	The Haunted House #2 R. A. Montgomery	$1.95
☐	15208	Sunken Treasure #3 E. Packard	$1.95
☐	15233	Your Very Own Robot #4 R. A. Montgomery	$1.95
☐	15308	Gorga, The Space Monster #5 E. Packard	$1.95
☐	15309	The Green Slime #6 S. Saunders	$1.95
☐	15195	Help! You're Shrinking #5 E. Packard	$1.95
☐	15201	Indian Trail #8 R. A. Montgomery	$1.95
☐	15191	The Genie In the Bottle #10 J. Razzi	$1.95
☐	15222	The Big Foot Mystery #11 L. Sonberg	$1.95
☐	15223	The Creature From Millers Pond #12 S. Saunders	$1.95
☐	15226	Jungle Safari #13 E. Packard	$1.95
☐	15227	The Search For Champ #14 S. Gilligan	$1.95

HARDCOVER EDITIONS

☐	05018	Sunken Treasure E. Packard	$6.95
☐	05019	Your Very Own Robot R. A. Montgomery	$6.95
☐	05031	Gorga, The Space Monster #5 E. Packard	$7.95
☐	05032	Green Slime #6 S. Saunders	$7.95

SPECIAL
MONEY SAVING
OFFER

Now you can have an up-to-date listing of Bantam's hundreds of titles plus take advantage of our unique and exciting bonus book offer. A special offer which gives you the opportunity to purchase a Bantam book for only 50¢. Here's how!

By ordering any five books at the regular price per order, you can also choose any other single book listed (up to a $4.95 value) for just 50¢. Some restrictions do apply, but for further details why not send for Bantam's listing of titles today!

Just send us your name and address plus 50¢ to defray the postage and handling costs.